OUROBOROS

BOOKS BY ANDREW DAVIE

Pavement
Ouroboros

ANDREW DAVIE

OUROBOROS

All Due Respect Books
an imprint of Down & Out Books
3959 Van Dyke Road, Suite 265
Lutz, FL 33558
DownAndOutBooks.com

Cover design by Zach McCain

ISBN: 1-64396-124-1
ISBN-13: 978-1-64396-124-8

For Chris

Sounds erupted throughout the cell blocks like a chamber orchestra rehearsing for a concert. The squeal of mattress springs, grunts, coughs, and other exhalations echoed off concrete walls. They accompanied the moans of all forms of sexual activity and the consumption of drugs which had been clandestinely transported from the outside world. Inmates licked magazine inserts, which had been dipped in acid, and snorted from balloons of heroin which had been smuggled in body cavities. People sipped fermented concoctions made from rotted fruit and sugar. Some inmates snored, others sang.

The prison library, however, was quiet. It had started as a single room with a few cardboard boxes full of used books. No one had remembered where they came from, or who brought them. One day there were three large cardboard boxes full of books, which had ranged from dime-store pulp fiction to academic textbooks on American history. Apparently, someone delivered them one year in the early

1950s and the prison had misplaced the inventory slip.

The following decade, during one of the more turbulent eras on college campuses, prison reform became a hot button issue. Students independently raised funds and helped to quadruple the number of books for the library. Some of the more determined students initiated a tutoring program that saw a few inmates receive their high school equivalency.

In the mid-1990s, the governor mandated another set of prison reforms. Though most of them had to do with hiring more guards, one such improvement was to overhaul the library. The new library consisted of two adjoining rooms, one which was solely dedicated to the housing of books and magazines. The other room had a computer and microfiche. The prison board had also created the position of a librarian to oversee the day-to-day operations. While this person would be an outside contractor, the rest of the staff would be hired from a pool of applicants from within the prison population.

The librarian had been working there for the last decade. He had probably been one of the same students who had embraced reform back in the sixties and had never given up the good fight. These days, when he was not helping convicts revise letters for their appeal, he was helping them learn how to read or reestablish communication with family members. He had a small office, but he was rarely there. Usually, he could be found pacing back and forth among the shelves clad in Birkenstocks and a short-sleeve button-down shirt. He'd gotten rid of his ponytail a few years previously.

Many of the jailhouse lawyers would use the library to meet with clients. These sessions occurred so often that the librarian had created a separate section. Twice a day, one of the convicts brought a cart down among the tiers to pass out and collect books; other duties consisted of cataloging and shelving books. These books, of course, had been screened before they made it to the shelves. The inmate who currently worked the library shift was Mark Franklin, though he never performed any of the job requirements.

At the start of his shift, he would punch in, sit down at one of the empty tables, and consume books. He had made arrangements with another inmate to push the cart on his behalf. Mark had been a high school dropout from upstate New York, so he had catch-up to do concerning his education. Once he got inside, he'd been reborn as an autodidact, and this was his time. Under the tutelage of the librarian, he set to work.

When Mark had gotten to prison, he was still

wet behind the ears about all matters. He didn't know anything about the unwritten rules and code of conduct which governed the microcosm of prison life. A week after he'd been processed, he had been out on the yard and noticed a few inmates gather nearby once he had begun his rotation at the bench press. In the end, he would never discover the reason for this particular attack.

Mark sat down on the bench, laid his head back on the cushion, and gripped the bar. His eyes caught some movement by his feet, and he noticed three men, now huddled together, were all looking in his direction. In another moment, all the other prisoners in Mark's vicinity had put down their equipment, moved away, and left him alone.

Without drawing attention to himself, Mark picked up a five-pound plate from the ground next to the bench. When the three men moved, he sat up and hurled it like a discus. It caught the first man in the shin, and he crumpled like a house of cards in the hands of a five-year-old. The man screamed in pain, and his cohorts attacked before Mark could initiate a second assault. He dodged the first incoming strike, a crudely assembled piece of rebar wrapped in duct tape. However, he was hit by the second—a toothbrush fashioned into a point. All the air left his lungs, and he sagged backward. On the ground, he stared at the object which protruded from his chest, bristle-side out. The sounds of riot guns broke through the white noise, and every man on the yard dropped to a push-up position. The man who'd been hit with the five-pound weight had suffered a broken tibia. The other two attackers had already disappeared back into the crowd of people. They had shrewdly discarded their weapons. Mark passed out. However, he had proven himself in the yard, and with that came a modicum of respect.

He was sent to the infirmary and prepped for surgery almost immediately. The recovery was a surreal experience. Time had passed, but he had almost no memory of the day's events. Now, suddenly, he was postoperative and decorated with rust-colored bandages. That first afternoon, once he was alert, an orderly came by and gave him a glass of water and some pills. Mark swallowed them and nearly choked when he drank the water.

"Easy," the orderly said. He was a large man with sleeves of tattoos and a shaved head with a thick Van Dyke.

"Don't worry, no one's going to come at you."

During that first year, Mark added a considerable amount of muscle to his frame. He no longer worried about getting ambushed while working out. He also learned how to protect himself more effectively should the need arise again. He studied Gray's Anatomy like it was the bible for effective ways to kill.

By the end of his third year, he would be directly responsible for the death of one other inmate. There hadn't been enough evidence for a conviction as the witness recanted his testimony. Over time, Mark became a respected member of the prison community. Though he stuck primarily with his own race, as mandated by the hierarchy, he got along well with everyone, prisoners and guards alike. He was most comfortable in his sanctuary in the library. The librarian had introduced him to a wide array of authors who wrote about themes which suited Mark's temperament. It was mostly crime fiction in the beginning, a lot of Mickey Spillane's Mike Hammer. Before long, he'd read *Being and Time* by Martin Heidegger, *The Collected Works of Henry David Thoreau*, and *The Count of Monte Cristo* by Andre Dumas. He'd studied the philosophy of Plato, Aristotle, Camus, Nietzsche, and devoured any other suggestions the librarian had had.

Now, a wiser and more astute Mark sat back in his chair and reflected on the last few years. Had he really ever been that obtuse? He had just learned the word's definition and was glad to find a use for it. He had just begun to read *The Aeneid* when he felt the presence of someone standing in the doorway nearby. He looked up and saw Don Parker.

"What?" He hated being interrupted when he'd started to read something, especially, if it wasn't for a good reason. With Don, it was never for a good reason.

"Hey, Mark," Don said. Sweat had already begun to drip from his nose.

"Don, it's like I told you," Mark said, sighed, and put the book on his knee. "Come back when you've got something to offer," Mark added.

He went back to reading his book.

Don licked his lips and wiped the sweat from his brow and nose. He started to walk away. Nausea pelted him in the stomach like the neighborhood kids who would mercilessly throw snowballs at him after the first snowfall. He hesitated in the hallway. Against all his judgment, he walked back inside the library.

Don wasn't built for prison. He didn't think he would be able to handle the daily grind.

His first day in the cafeteria a fight broke out at the next table, and Don watched a man get stabbed in the face with a fork four times. That night he cried uncontrollably into his pillow. He prayed no one else would be able to hear him, but the remarks about his breakdown were audible almost immediately after it had started. He knew he needed to pull it together, or he wouldn't survive.

The following days had been mirror images of his first, and it reiterated he wouldn't last long. It was a foreign world, and he felt he could be killed at any time. He assumed the pressure would eventually cause him to go crazy. Not to mention, he had all the time in the world to think about the mistakes he had made. He found an outlet, though.

Most days, he walked around under the influence of heroin. If he was stoned, he wasn't as inclined to worry about the never-ending peril. The problem would always occur after he'd come down from his high. He'd managed to avoid having problematic withdrawals, but he knew it was only a matter of time before they began. He'd seen the effects firsthand. Most convicts in withdrawal had transferred out of his unit and were slowly dying in the hospital. To avoid that same outcome, there were some rules Don had sworn to adhere to from the beginning. So far, he had stuck with them. He wouldn't shoot it. No matter how many times people said it was better than multiple orgasms. He would only snort it. True, it burned, and he was probably destroying his sinuses, but he could deal with that.

Worse was his tolerance kept getting greater. Don snapped from his memory and spoke.

"Maybe there is something," Don said.

Mark put the book down. The look he had on his face suggested he'd better be dazzled by Don's sudden revelation.

"I was a teacher on the outside. Maybe, I could help you with what you're reading?" Don approached Mark tentatively, as one would a wounded but still dangerous animal. Mark lifted the book and rotated it, so it appeared to be dancing in his hands.

"Non postulo vestri auxilium," he said.

Don stopped walking. The forced smile disappeared from his face.

"It's Latin, Don. It means 'I don't need your help.'"

Don felt like he had been crushed beneath a wave. He almost started to cry, but he held himself together. He turned to leave and had made it to the doorway when he heard Mark call him back.

"Wait a second," Mark began. "There might be something after all."

A few hours later, Don was on his way to Mark's cell. He tried to walk with a determined gait, but he knew he looked foolish, so he slowed down. A kid stood outside of Mark's cell. For some reason, he reminded Don of a crossing guard. The kid put his hand out for Don to hold up. Rail thin, the kid looked barely out of his teens, and his prison-issue hung off his bony frame. He tried to exude menace by keeping his brow furrowed, but it just gave him a confused look instead. Regardless, Don wasn't going to try him.

"Yeah, Mark sent for me," Don said.

The kid looked him up and down and called out over his shoulder.

"Hey, you got someone here," the kid said.

"Who?" Mark's voice boomed from inside his cell.

"It's Don," Don answered.

The kid's face quickly spun back, and he stared at Don. He furrowed his eyebrows some more, which Don didn't think was possible.

"Come inside," Mark replied.

The kid looked like he wanted to say something but stayed quiet. He made a motion for Don to continue, and Don walked into the cell. Mark sat shirtless on the bottom bunk. A tattoo artist was sticking him with the hollow tube of a Bic pen which had been fitted with the high E of a guitar string. An AC adapter had been jury-rigged from an old Walkman to act as the motor. Don watched as the artist dipped the needle into a toothpaste cap full of black ink and traced the outline. Don squirmed when the thoughts of hygiene entered his mind, and he wondered whether Mark had contracted some form of hepatitis or worse. Don couldn't help but imagine sores which would open up on Mark's body later like flower buds reaching maturity.

The artist wiped at Mark's shoulder with a towel and dipped the needle into a Dixie cup of red water. Each cup contained water with a different colored M&M. As the candy shells dissolved, they would provide the colors needed for Mark's tattoo. Don watched the man work for another minute. The work was of a snake eating its own tail. The artist finished shading, put the machine down, and told Mark he was done. Mark thanked him for his time and gave him a few packs of smokes. The artist dressed his work with Vaseline, collected his gear, and left the cell. Mark and Don were alone.

Mark looked at the design, then stood up, and went over to the bars. He whispered to the kid who had remained the entire time. Keeping watch while someone got tattooed was known as "sitting jiggers." It was a way the kid could start to curry favor with people. When the kid confirmed they were in the clear, Mark returned to his bunk and removed a homemade knife from underneath his mattress.

"Someone will slip you one of these," Mark said

and handed the weapon to Don.

Don held the weapon in his hand. He marveled at its weight. The severity of his situation brought him back to reality, and he almost backed out of their agreement. But he didn't. This is the only way, he reminded himself; he would have protection from here on out and a steady supply of heroin to boot.

"You'll probably only get one good shot with it, so I'd go for the carotid artery here." Mark pointed to the side of his neck.

"I want you to practice," Mark said.

"What?" Don's head shot up.

"On me," Mark said and took a step back to give them some more space.

Don gripped the piece of fiberglass in his hand. It felt cold and unforgiving. His whole body shook.

"Let's go," Mark said.

Impatience had begun to creep into his voice.

"On you?" Don's words barely escaped his lips. He thought he was going to lose control of his bowels.

"How else are you going to learn?" Mark's tone changed again. This time it sounded to Don like a surprise.

"The key is to jab it in a motion like this," Mark said as he took the weapon from Don and demonstrated the action. His motion was fluid, and he stopped the blade just before it met with Don's neck. Don was in awe of how close Mark had come to stabbing him. Don took the weapon back from Mark, but he hesitated. If he were to accidentally hit Mark, it would mean the end. Die immediately; do not collect two hundred dollars. Meet your maker as a result of stabbing a man who had an insurance policy with one of the most notorious gangs in the prison. Don took a deep breath and tried his best to mimic what he'd just seen. He swung his arm in the same motion, and he had delivered what appeared to be a killing blow.

"Good, that's exactly it!" Mark said and slapped Don on the back.

"Now do it again," Mark added.

Don felt some of the color return to his face. He took a step to the side and executed the move again. This time, after he had finished, Mark grabbed Don's shoulder and squeezed. Don felt the camaraderie between the two of them, which hadn't been there before. They enacted the scene a few more times as if they had been rehearsing for a Shakespearean drama. The lookout signaled them, and they refrained until the guard had passed. When they finished, Don's shirt was nearly soaked through. Though he was still revved up with anxiety, he tried his best not to let it show.

"That's good," Mark said.

He produced a smoke, lit the end, and sat back on his bunk. Don continued to stare at the weapon in the middle of the cell.

"You're going to be doing something really important," Mark said and blew out a smoke ring.

"Thanks," Don said.

The bell went off. Lockdown was about to begin.

"Listen," Mark began, "I want you to practice when you have the chance."

"I will."

Don returned the weapon to Mark, who slipped it under the mattress. He darted back to his cell. Along the way, he felt the strength return to his body. He walked with his head up, and his stride had a snap to it.

Among others, protective custody housed snitches, pedophiles, informants, and former peace officers who had been sentenced. Essentially, it was made up of people who had to fear for their lives. The Protective Custody Unit was segregated from the general population. Ryan O'Sullivan had just stretched out on the top bunk and interlaced his fingers behind his head. Before he knew it, he'd fallen asleep. He awoke to the sound of the bars in the cell opening.

He rolled over and watched two COs push a prisoner inside. The prisoner shuffled back against the bars once they closed and allowed the COs to undo his manacles.

O'Sullivan's new cellmate moved with nervous energy like an addict who had started going through withdrawals. O'Sullivan quickly recognized the man posed no threat, so he relaxed a bit. Even if his celly found out O'Sullivan used to be a cop, and it rubbed him the wrong way, it didn't appear he would be able to do anything about it. The guy was probably a short eyes—a child molester. They made up the bulk of convicts in protective custody, along with snitches. Former cops, like O'Sullivan, were rare.

Aside from looking like he wanted to jump out of his skin, his new cellmate probably weighed one hundred twenty pounds soaking wet. Casually, O'Sullivan rolled over the edge of the bunk and descended to the floor.

"I never thought I'd say this but—" he had begun to say but stopped midway through his sentence. The other prisoner had stabbed him in the neck.

Don didn't think he would be able to do it. He was hyperventilating when he got into the cell. He assumed the guards thought he was scared. Don knew he'd be adding time to his sentence with what he was about to do, but Mark had told him if he pleaded self-defense, it would work to his favor. O'Sullivan would be dead and wouldn't be able to mount any contrary arguments. Not to mention, while there were cameras on the unit, if he stayed near the cell door he'd be in a partial blind spot.

O'Sullivan rolled off the top bunk and onto the floor. It was now or never. Don gripped the handle of the weapon. He remembered to stay close to the cell door. O'Sullivan was in reach. He started to speak. Don struck. However, Don hadn't been able to get a good momentum going. He had to adjust his killing stroke. Instead of hooking the blade as he'd practiced, he drove it straight up. It sliced the side of O'Sullivan's neck. Don went for a second blow but O'Sullivan had backed away. Don wouldn't leave the protection of the blind spot. He watched O'Sullivan sag to the floor as crimson began to flow through his fingers. O'Sullivan retched once. He tried to rise but stumbled back further into the cell. Don dropped the knife and vomited at the sight of the geyser which had erupted from the side of O'Sullivan's neck.

Mark Franklin had gotten the news later that

evening: Ryan O'Sullivan, the former cop, was now dead. He'd succumbed to blood loss before they could get him stitched up. Mark reacted by keeping a calm exterior, but on the inside he was ecstatic. Ryan O'Sullivan's assailant, Don Parker, would not be able to reveal to anyone why he had attacked O'Sullivan. When the deed was over, Don had sat cross-legged on the ground near the cell door. Two prisoners walked by protective custody in quick succession. One of them pushed a mop and bucket on wheels. They paused momentarily outside of the cell. The first one squirted cleaning fluid through the bars, and the second one with the mop and bucket threw in a match.

"Burnt to a crisp." The man who had sought out Mark to relay the information continued. "They're still peeling him off the floor."

The man spat a golden brown glob of tobacco juice into a cup he had removed from his pants pocket.

That takes care of that, thought Mark. He gave the man a fist bump and thanked him for relaying the message. He could celebrate later.

Gropper heard the noise of clothes rustling in the closet, and it confirmed his suspicions. He opened the door. She had tried to hide among the coats, but she hadn't done a good job of concealing herself.

"No fair," she said. "You cheated."

Gropper wanted to tell her he hadn't cheated. She had made too much noise, but he had come to realize it was almost impossible to reason with a six-year-old, especially one with such a passion for playing hide and seek.

"Let's play again!" she said and clapped her hands together. She stayed wedged between two coats but she continued to have difficulty. However, she seemed to have already forgotten having accused Gropper of cheating only seconds before that. The fact she had still wanted to play hide and seek when they had been at it for two hours already was also something he had trouble reconciling. His beeper went off, though, which saved him from having to embark on another round. Liz heard the beeper and her face became sullen.

"That means you've got to go, right?" she said.

"Yes," Gropper said.

He'd been living with Liz and her mother Connie for a few months now. He had missed staying at Miss Bradley's place; she had had quite the vinyl collection, and most of the time there would be jazz playing in the background. Plus, Miss Bradley, then in her advanced age, wouldn't pester him to play hide and seek.

However, Gropper knew he could never go back there. Whether or not the cartel would seek revenge after Gropper had interfered with their business remained to be seen, but he couldn't chance it. So, instead, McGill had set him up with another relative of a former client. Connie was a nurse, recently divorced, who worked constantly, so she had jumped at the chance to have Gropper around. Liz, her daughter, had taken some more convincing, but she came around pretty quickly after Gropper had demonstrated not only his prowess for hide and seek, but also his willingness to play. McGill had told them Gropper usually worked nights, and this would be just a temporary arrangement, but for now, it suited everyone.

Gropper told Liz they could finish their game tomorrow. She had begun to argue with him, but as usual, she quickly lost interest when she realized her mother would be home soon. Gropper watched her emerge from under the coats, race from the closet of her bedroom, and into the living room. She would spend the next half an hour reading quietly and waiting for her mother's key to hit the lock.

After she had left the room, Gropper looked at his beeper and read the coded message from McGill.

* * *

Like most other states, the South Carolina Board of Paroles and Pardons was made up of seven people from different congressional districts who had been appointed by the governor. This group was comprised of former lawyers, judges, and therapists, who had the power to grant, modify, or deny parole. They would consider all sorts of things before they rendered their verdict. If there had been a victim, some cases would hinge completely on the victim's testimony. It didn't matter whether the inmate had found redemption or been a model prisoner. Mark knew of convicts whose victims would send in videos every year which included a detailed account of how they still suffered physically and emotionally and would bear the psychological scars of the event for the rest of their lives.

Convicts on the receiving end of one of those videos never had a chance. Some of them had given up the thought of ever getting paroled, so they attempted to adjust to life behind bars for the next twenty to thirty years. In some cases, they might never see the outside again.

Luckily for Mark, he wouldn't have to endure one of those videos.

Earlier that morning, Mark had showered and

shaved. He dressed in newly ironed prison issue, but he still felt he looked like a felon. It didn't matter, though, just as long as the board saw someone deserving of parole. He would probably have to discuss details of the murder he'd been accused of. It would be difficult but having the testimony against him recanted was in his favor.

After he had a chance to eat breakfast, he and a few other inmates, who were also up for parole, were led to a hallway outside of a conference room. One at a time, each of them would go inside and video chat with the parole board. Mark didn't know how many people had been in the queue before him, or how many people were going to go through the motions afterward. He took a seat on the bench in the hallway and tried not to think about the manacles, which had already begun to chafe his ankles and wrists. He turned his thoughts to business.

They were going bury Don Parker's charred remains today. Don's incarceration had made him such a pariah to his family that no one had claimed the body for a private burial. He became a ward of the state so plans were quickly put into motion for Don to spend the rest of eternity in the prison's cemetery located about half a mile away. O'Sullivan's family had claimed his body and made preparations to ship him home. Mark wondered what would happen when it was his turn to go. Both of his parents and his brother were dead. He had no other family to speak of, either. Would he wind up in some little known cemetery near a prison grounds?

Gropper had taken a different route to the diner. It was probably not necessary, but it helped to keep him sharp. He didn't particularly care for the place, but McGill seemed to have an affinity for it; probably why the man had made it his office.

They had been working together for about a little over two years now, and the partnership suited both of their sensibilities. McGill would handle the client-side, take all the adulation, and have as many pancakes, burgers, and coffee as he wanted, free of charge. Normally, he could drink all the Mickeys he'd wanted, but he'd cut them out after his last visit to the doctor.

Gropper would address the backend work. He didn't want any praise. He had become accustomed to operating out of sight, which was the way he preferred it. Gropper looked over his shoulder one more time out of habit, but no one was there.

Inside, the place was bustling as it always was. McGill was seated at "his table." He had given up using a booth a few months back and requisitioned a table in the back of the diner near the pay phones. When Gropper walked in, McGill had been working on a stack of pancakes, a side of bacon, and who knows which number cup of coffee. He would start drinking the stuff early in the morning and never stop for the entire day. He was the only person Gropper knew who could drink coffee at night and wouldn't be affected by the caffeine. Lord knows what the man's digestive track looked like. The fact the doctor's only suggestion was to cut back on the alcohol had been a miracle. Gropper walked through tables of families and people who'd had that morning's newspaper spread out until he got to McGill's table.

"Have a seat," McGill said.

Gropper did so. Whatever was on McGill's mind must have been important because he had chosen to avoid leading with the usual banter. One of the waiters had spotted Gropper, came over, and placed a green tea in front of him.

"Thank you," Gropper said.

The waiter nodded and made haste. Basil, the owner, had instructed the staff about McGill's use of the diner as his office, so they left him alone during his time there. Except for when they brought him food or coffee, he was essentially a ghost. Occasionally, one of the wait staff would answer the phone if it rang, but ninety-nine percent of the time it would prove to be a client for McGill, so they would let him answer the phone himself.

"We got something new," McGill said. He went on to reveal the details. Jennifer or "Diamond" was a college student who had been dancing at a gentleman's club to make ends meet. She felt safe while inside working since the place had a solid staff of bouncers. However, it was when she left she felt unsettled. A few nights in a row while walking to her car, she caught one of the regulars following her. She had brought the matter up to her boss, but the guy said once she left the property it was out of his hands.

"She wants us to put the fear into him."

"I understand," Gropper said. He started to rise when McGill motioned for him to stay.

"There's one more thing. Ryan O'Sullivan was murdered," McGill said.

Mark had been born the second child to Mary and Charles Franklin, and from what he'd gathered early on, he had not been planned. His brother Steve was almost a decade older than him. Regardless of the age difference, though, the brothers had been close. Of course, Steve had left home before Mark turned eight, but Mark always had fond memories of the things they would do together when he still lived at home. Steve had taught Mark how to hunt, fish, and play sports. Steve had essentially become Mark's father since their own father barely had time for anything other than working on the farm. They lived in a small town in upstate New York with a population of under five hundred. Mark had always been a wild kid and, although not a troublemaker, needed to be disciplined more often than not. He spent the majority of his time imagining a world outside of the confines of his small town. When he was seventeen, Mark decided that, similar to his brother, he would escape from the monotony. Had he stayed, he would have taken over the family farm like all his friends. He wasn't keen on the idea of working as a farmer. He'd never really taken to it; he reluctantly did his chores and helped out when he could, but he was destined for bigger things. What really scared him was the thought he'd succumb to the boredom. He was convinced it was the boredom which had been the true cause of death for most people under the age of fifty he'd known. Two of his friends had died in drunk driving accidents. Another had committed suicide by lying down on the train tracks. The train ran through, but it didn't stop in the town. Three people, a quarter of his graduating class, had died before their time. It was enough to get him thinking that maybe this town wasn't the best place for him to spend the remainder of his life. Not to mention there was the situation with Emma Van Rood. They hadn't been together for long, but she had confided in him she was late in having her period. This would have spelled disaster for certain since her father was a preacher. She'd kept things quiet for now, but who knows how long that would last? If what she said was true, not only would she have sullied her family name, but Mark would definitely be roped into a shotgun wedding. Hell, he'd seen it before with at least two others in his graduating class of eleven. He'd be damned if he was going to let that happen to him, though. It was one thing to navigate life here on his own, and it would be another to have to provide for "Mrs. Emma Franklin."

"You're going to get caught." Aaron had said and cracked open another beer. He was a simple-minded oaf who towered over most people. Many in the town knew him as a gentle giant. At six foot six, he always had a permanent blank stare on his face which only served to re-enforce the stereotype. One time, he tried to open a car door and pulled hard enough to ruin the alignment. He was Mark's best friend and obeyed anything Mark said like it was ordered from The Almighty.

"I'm not going to get caught," Mark had responded and let out a loud belch. They were on the outskirts of town, in the parking lot of a revival campground, leaning up against the grill of Aaron's car, staring off into trees. It was a favorite spot for them as they could carry on their business unobserved. There was too much undergrowth for deer to navigate, so hunters stayed clear. There wasn't a scheduled revival for weeks. He polished off his beer, crushed the can, and tossed it into the woods. What did Aaron know? Mark had a plan, and it was going to work. He was going to get out of this town. He didn't want to argue, though, because it would mean having to explain everything from the beginning, and he had already done that twice. He and Aaron drank another few, and Aaron dropped Mark off at his house. Mark hugged his friend goodbye and told him he would keep in touch when he got settled. Aaron seemed shaken, but he didn't say anything further.

As someone who'd returned home late many a night, Mark knew the creak in each step and was able to maneuver without making too much noise to alert his parents. When he got to his room, he shut the door behind him and turned on the light. His stuff was already packed and rested near the foot of his bed. He walked over to the closet and removed a black case from the back. He unzipped it and took out a shotgun. He and his brother had gone hunting in the woods behind their house, and after Steve had departed, it had been Mark and Aaron. Last year Mark had taken a six-point buck. He hefted the weapon and checked the action. He had already cleaned and oiled it, as he knew that it might see use tomorrow, though he hoped not.

That night he slept soundly and had no dreams. It would be the last good night's sleep he'd get for some time, he reckoned. Mark awoke at five that morning, wrote a note for his parents stating he was leaving and never coming back. He thought it'd have been a more difficult letter to pen, but the words flowed from him effortlessly. He gathered his belongings and crossed the threshold of his doorway for the last time.

The weather that morning was crisp. He buttoned his coat to the top and put on a knit wool cap. He got in his car, his high school graduation present, a down payment for his future as a farmer, and drove away. Mark coasted for a few minutes until he arrived at his destination. He pulled the car into the general store's small parking lot.

Ben Townsend owned the place; he had since Mark could remember. It was a last chance stop before the highway, and it was where most of the teenagers convened to pick up smokes and beer before they headed out to the wilderness. Mark kept the motor running and stepped out of the car into the brisk wind. He took one last deep breath to settle his nerves, turned, and picked up the shotgun from the passenger side seat.

Ben was a likable guy, in his fifties, who had seen Mark and his friends grow up from rowdy little kids into young adults. Mark had always liked Ben. When Mark had gone to the store as a youngster, Ben had always given him a candy bar. As he grew older, Ben would look the other way if Mark bought a pack of smokes; something Mark's father had frowned upon. According to Ben, if Mark wanted to smoke it was fine by him, as long as he kept leading the football team to victory. However, today his affection for Ben would not get in the way of his plans.

He entered the store only after he was sure they would be alone. Mark had slung the shotgun over his shoulder. Ben wouldn't think it peculiar. It was hunting season, and the general store also doubled as an ammunition shop. Ben was drinking coffee and reading one of the fishing magazines.

"Hey, Mark," he said when he saw the young man approaching.

"How's it going, Ben?"

"Pretty well, what can I do for you this morning?

Mark brought the case down onto the counter and rested the weapon on top of it. Ben swiveled in his chair, reached into a cardboard box behind him, and touched a box of shells. It was at that point he heard Mark slide the pump of the Winchester. He turned around. Mark had raised the weapon. It was sighted on Ben's chest.

"Ben, take it real easy. I don't want to shoot you. I just need everything from the register, and I'm gone."

Ben tried to say something, but the words would not come. Mark looked down at his watch. He'd only been in there for less than a minute. Ben slowly rose from his seat. He walked the few feet to the register, pulled the arm, and released the cash register's tray. He lifted each of the weights and took the bills out. Mark wiped his nose. The sweat was now noticeable through his shirt even though the temperature wouldn't have called for it. It didn't matter. In a few more seconds, he'd have the money and be able to start his new life. Mark had just snatched the money from Ben's hand, wiped his brow, and turned to go when he saw Henry Johansson was about to walk into the store. Shit.

* * *

Police Chief Henry Johansson had pulled into the general store parking lot as he always did before he went to the station. It was how he started every day. He'd get coffee and talk with Ben Townsend. They would discuss anything, though, it would usually turn back to reflecting about their glory days from high school. Henry eased out of the driver's side door, adjusted his belt, sidearm, and Stetson, and walked into the store. At one point, he stopped to pick up his pants from around his waist since they were prone to slip. He sauntered toward the counter where Ben and Mark Franklin were.

"Ben, I hope you haven't run out of coffee; I'm in dire straits this morning," Henry said.

Ben didn't respond. He looked like he was in some sort of trance.

"Ben?"

"Yeah, I'm fine," Ben managed.

"Let me get you some coffee," he added.

Ben hurried away to fetch the pot as Henry squared up to the counter. He looked the boy up and down. Mark smiled and nodded.

"Sir," Mark said.

"Ain't you supposed to be in school this morning?" Henry said.

Mark swallowed hard.

"I am; you got me. I was just hoping to get some

shells for this afternoon."

Henry looked at the shotgun which lay on top of the case.

"Winchester, huh? I used to have one myself," Henry said. He picked up the gun from the counter, aimed the weapon toward the ground, looked down the sight, and feigned pulling the trigger. He handed the weapon back to Mark.

"Well, you better hurry on over to the school. And watch out for the middle linebacker at South Otselic on Friday."

"Thank you, sir," Mark said. He began to walk toward the front door, but Henry called out after him.

"Mark."

He stopped.

"Yes, sir?"

"If you get one of them bucks, let me know. I'm always in the mood for venison."

"You got it."

McGill had gone through most of the particulars with Gropper. Someone had convinced a recently transferred prisoner to attack O'Sullivan in protective custody. Once McGill had heard the details of assassin's background, he knew it hadn't been spontaneous. This was not a crime of passion. It had to have been premeditated, and someone else had been pulling the strings.

"The guy was a nonviolent offender, and from what I read he was scared of his own shadow," McGill said. So far, it was just a theory since there had been no real evidence. But once the general population found out O'Sullivan had been a cop? McGill thought it would just be a matter of time before word made it to the wrong people. Worse, it could have been someone out for revenge.

"Things are well, otherwise?" McGill said. He forked another strip of bacon into his mouth and chewed.

"She's getting better at hide and seek," Gropper said.

Gropper had been apprehensive about moving in with Connie and Liz. It wasn't that he disliked kids, but he hadn't been around them much. He didn't know how well the arrangement would work.

"But she's still not that good, right?" McGill said.

"No."

Slowly, and without rushing into it, he and McGill would go into the plan for how to prepare in case O'Sullivan's murder was just the beginning of a vendetta. If O'Sullivan had been killed by someone looking for revenge, they might make a play for

McGill, since O'Sullivan had been McGill's partner early in his career on the force. While it certainly made things more complicated, since McGill could be found most days at the diner, Gropper was up for the challenge. It allowed him to test his mettle. Again, this was how he had preferred it.

McGill put his hand up in the air for more coffee, and a waiter came by with a pot. Once he was refilled, he continued to work on his stack of pancakes.

"Let's say it is someone with a grudge. I would assume they're going to get eyes on this place if they haven't already?" McGill said.

"Absolutely."

"Franklin," the guard said and broke Mark from his daydream. Mark shifted, felt his manacles constrict and looked at the other two convicts who shared his bench. One of them was asleep. The other had leaned back as far as his chains would allow and stared at the ceiling. This was Mark's second time up for parole. The first time, he had no idea about the procedure. Now, even though it was only his second time, he felt much more comfortable. The guard instructed Mark to stand and led him into the room.

The previous time he'd gone through the process Mark figured the more sincere he could act the better it would look. Afterward, he'd realized it didn't matter as long as he wasn't openly hostile. Later that first evening, long after his meeting had taken place, he came to the conclusion the parole board had already made up their minds before the session had begun. The way the convict presented himself during the conference would merely confirm or deny their initial decision.

The room doubled as a storage, but all the items it housed had been pushed to one side. The video camera and monitor were already on and aimed in the direction of a folding chair, placed against the far wall. Mark took his seat and stared at the monitor. All members of the parole board looked tired; like they had been at it for a few hours already. The sense of unpleasantness was visible in the stoop of their postures, or the look in their eyes. Each of them had a folder open on the table. The only way he could be denied, he figured, was if they focused on—

"Mr. Franklin?" a bored-looking man with male pattern baldness and thick glasses said. He must be the foreman.

"Yes, sir?"

"Let's begin, shall we?"

"I'm ready whenever you are, sir."

Each member of the parole board asked questions in order which had ranged from problems in Mark's youth to his current employment in the library. It took him a moment, but he settled down and found a rhythm with their questions. The librarian had written a letter recommending Mark for parole. He had also testified earlier to Mark's capabilities and hard work he'd done in the prison library. The kind words didn't even cost Mark anything; the librarian had been willing to do it of his own accord. Mark was looking forward to answering questions about his future, and whether he would pose a threat if they reintegrated him into society.

"Can you fill us in on the details behind the death of Mr. Clint Selridge?" one of them asked.

Shit.

Gropper had made sure to get home after Liz had gone to sleep. He wasn't up for another game of hide and seek. Connie, however, was up and enjoying a glass of wine when Gropper let himself into the apartment. He missed having his own entrance as he had in his previous place, but he was adjusting as best as he could to this new arrangement.

Connie lifted her glass in recognition of his arrival and took a sip. She had changed out of her scrubs, and it looked like she had showered as well. She was in sweats, which Gropper had learned meant she was not going to go out later that evening. On previous occasions, she and her friends would meet up somewhere in the neighborhood. Once, she had invited Gropper to join them. She said it wouldn't be a problem to find a sitter, but Gropper had declined. She had never asked again. Gropper went into the kitchen, put the kettle on the stove, returned to the living room, and sat in one of the chairs diagonally across from Connie. She had been aware of the working relationship Gropper had with McGill, but in the beginning, she had been curious about the arrangement.

"So, you're his retainer—sort of like a samurai?" she had said. It had caught Gropper off guard at the time since he didn't expect her to be familiar with samurai or their code. It was a mistake he wouldn't make again.

"In a way," Gropper began, "I could explain it, and you would understand in theory. But it would be similar to describing what it's like to be in combat to someone whose never been to war."

She had understood, and she had appreciated his candor. They continued to speak for a while, and she got sidetracked with a story about a kid who'd come in earlier that day with a ruptured brain aneurysm.

"He had been at the airport at the time and passed out on the jetway. Luckily for him, it was in the morning, so the first responders were able to get there immediately."

"What happened?"

"He's in the ICU now." She paused to collect her thoughts. "It's funny, everything which could have gone wrong for him did, but everything which could have broken his way also did."

"Like yin and yang," Gropper said.

They had toasted their respective drinks at the time. It was at that point she and Gropper had started to become friends. He learned she had taught in Japan before becoming a nurse and had an affinity for Asian culture, as he had.

Now, she looked exhausted and weary on the couch. It must have been a rough day, but Gropper wasn't going to intrude. If she wanted to open up, she would, but he wouldn't prompt her. It didn't appear as if she wanted to talk about work, though, which was also fine by him. They continued to sit together in silence.

Mark had been accused of killing Clint Selridge, and even though the witness had later recanted his testimony, it had stained Mark's record. This time, the question had been asked by an overweight man in a burgundy suit who sat a few places away from the foreman. Mark had been prepared for this question, but at the same time, he had hoped somehow it would have gotten lost in the shuffle. Deep down, he knew it was going to be impossible to avoid. They would want to discuss the incident.

Selridge had been a large man; not muscular, but he had been able to handle himself and he moved surprisingly quickly. He had come to Mark's cell and told him there was a convict from another cellblock who had accused Mark of ripping him off. He was also saying things which were damaging to Mark's reputation. Mark had still been green enough to believe the story. Selridge had assured Mark he needed to handle the situation before it got out of control. Selridge had even offered to accompany Mark, and he would help him deal with the matter.

Mark had discovered later this hadn't been the first time Selridge had run this confidence game on a new prisoner. In fact, it was his bread and butter. Of course, the entire story had been a fabrication.

The plan had been to get Mark on to the upper tier of this particular cell block and follow him up there. Mark figured Selridge had estimated, at that particular time of day, since it was a remote unit with limited supervision, he could take advantage of a new convict and satisfy some of his urges. Selridge's accomplice, a runty-looking fellow named Williamson, had already been in place as the lookout. His instructions had been simple: run interference if anyone else tried to get on the tier, or signal Selridge should a hack try to investigate. The plan was so simple even Williamson could handle it.

However, as he followed Mark, closed the distance, and was only an arm's length away, Mark heard a sound behind him. He spun around and hit Selridge in the stomach. Selridge let out an oof and slunk to the ground. The anticipation had gotten the better of him, and as a result, he gave himself away.

While he was on the ground and unable to defend himself, Mark straddled him, gripped a fistful of his hair, and proceeded to cave in Selridge's skull. Initially, "Willy" as Williamson had been called, turned the corner, saw what was happening, and froze. Mark locked eyes with Willy, who backed away with his hands raised.

Later, when Selridge's body was discovered, Willy, accused Mark of the crime. Statements were taken from both men, and a hearing was scheduled for Willy to testify. Mark denied the accusation altogether. However, before the administration could move Willy to protective custody, someone visited Willy on Mark's behalf.

The man, who Mark had paid, explained to Willy that if he went through with his testimony, he would eventually regret it. Mark could afford to be patient with him. Willy would be looking over his shoulder for as long as Mark was in prison. It was enough to get Willy to change his mind, and although the administration was up in arms, there was nothing they could do. Willy would claim he was mistaken in his identification of Mark, and the charges would be dropped. Eventually, the matter got lost in the shuffle altogether.

Once the parole board was satisfied they had exhausted the details of Selridge's death to their satisfaction, and Mark had continued to deny any knowledge of it, they proceeded with the interview. Mark answered the rest of the parole board's questions, which were tame by comparison.

About the crime that landed him in prison, did he feel remorse for his actions?

"Yes, ma'am," Mark said.

Would he be a productive member of society should he get paroled?

"Yes, sir," he said.

That was the last question.

"Very well," the balding foreman finally said. "Unless anyone has any further questions?" He paused and eyed the panel. When no one spoke, he banged a gavel on the table.

"Thank you, Mr. Franklin."

"Thank you, sir," Mark said.

The monitor flicked off, and Mark sat alone in the darkness of the room. A moment went by, the door opened, and the guard entered. Mark stood, adjusted his manacles, and the guard led him to the hallway.

McGill had kept two photos in his wallet. By now, each had white lines crisscrossing through them, and the finish had been worn away. One of them was of Renee, his former CI, and friend, who'd passed away. Someone had taken it when she was in graduate school. She had been seated at a desk with different reference books opened to various pages. She had looked good. She smiled in the photo. It was before she had turned to the bottle. The other photo was of McGill and O'Sullivan early in his career. O'Sullivan had been the senior partner back then, responsible for hipping McGill to the ways of the job. The photo hadn't been taken directly after his graduation from the academy, but it might have been in the first year he had been on the force. McGill had looked much different back then. It wasn't just because he weighed less. He hadn't yet been burdened by experience.

McGill put the photos down on the table and took a drink of coffee.

He spent some time recollecting the details of the more high-profile cases he and O'Sullivan had worked, but he knew it was a waste of time. O'Sullivan hadn't been on everyone's shit list, but he was exactly a choirboy either.

Mark had been in the library when he got word he had been granted parole. He had been re-reading *The Aeneid*. He had just read his favorite part. Aeneas and his men have been through Hell. They have lived through the sacking of their home, Troy, and now while on a voyage to fulfill a prophecy have endured a horrible situation at sea. Aeneas tries to console them by saying "Someday, perhaps, remembering even this will be a pleasure." Mark put the book down to reflect on that concept when his proxy with the cart returned to the library. The man looked more animated than usual, and it wasn't because he had just shot up. He had caught wind of the information while pushing the cart. He had cut his route short, so he could come back with the news. Mark was going to get parole.

Jesse stared through the glass partition and waited for her client. She had completed all facets of the Department of Probation, Parole, and Pardon Services' basic training program years ago but being in a prison still hadn't lost its effect on her. Anyone could learn about safety training, how to handle a firearm, pressure point tactics, and Effective Practices in Correctional Settings, but there had been nothing in the training to deal with what it would feel like to have a three-hundred-pound serial rapist stare at you from the other side of the glass.

She popped in another Nicorette lozenge. She had to remind herself not to chew it. She hadn't craved a cigarette, and she had realized a few days ago she was probably done with them. However, she had simply traded in her smoking habit for a lozenge habit. It was a never-ending cycle like most things in life; a similar pitfall to how her clients would fall back into their criminal activities.

The door on the other side opened, and Mark Franklin walked through. She recognized him from his booking photo. She has spent the last few days familiarizing herself with the details of his case so she could help him transition once he got on the outside. Mark took the seat and picked up the phone. Jesse picked up hers.

"I'm Jesse Ames," she said. "I'll be your PO. And yes, I know, like the gunslinger. Trust me, I've heard them all before."

They spoke for about twenty minutes. She was no-nonsense, which he appreciated. Overweight but muscular, wearing tight clothes, but most importantly, she seemed to have retained a lot of idealism. He could tell by how she conducted herself during the conversation, and the points she made. She had reminded him of the librarian, which he welcomed. Jesse had gone over the details of his parole plan including his need to reside in a halfway house, or what was now referred to as an RRC, or residential re-entry center. She had also gotten him a job working as a custodian at a library, which had piqued his interest. As their conversation wound down, she told him about the few hundred dollars he would get in "gate money" when he was discharged and that she would meet him at her office a few days after he was out on parole. They could go over everything else in more depth at that point. They both hung up their phones. She popped what looked like gum into her mouth and left the room. Franklin stood. He didn't even wait to be summoned by the guard. On his way back to his cell, he began thinking of other arrangements he'd have to make upon his release.

Gropper listened intently to Bill Evans's improvisation on the piano. Miles Davis had once commented about Evans's playing: "He played the piano the way it's supposed to be played." Gropper could only follow along in awe. He'd been parked across the street from Scott Baker's place of work, the man who had been making "Diamond" the dancer, Jennifer, feel uncomfortable. Gropper continued to listen as the rest of the band came back in and accompanied Bill Evans on piano.

The shops in the neighborhood were starting to shut down for the evening, which meant Baker was due to follow suit and come outside soon. He worked at an electronics repair shop, as a shift supervisor. Gropper watched him emerge from the back office, turn off the light, and walk outside. He locked the front door and said goodnight to a sales associate from a neighboring boutique who was also locking up. The other person said good night, departed down the sidewalk and left Baker alone.

Baker was middle-aged, about fifty pounds over-weight. He had an awful combover. When Baker had finished with the door, he stayed in the entryway and took out his phone. He started to scroll through messages. Gropper exited his vehicle, shut the door behind him, and after he paused to let a few cars go by crossing the street.

"Mr. Baker?" Gropper said after he'd gotten a few feet away.

Baker lifted his head and scrutinized Gropper. "Yes?"

Gropper hit him in the stomach. He didn't wind up, so as not to attract attention, but the punch still did the job. Baker wheezed and coughed. He had also dropped his phone. Gropper picked up the phone and guided Baker further back into the entryway, so they were both hidden from passersby.

"Just catch your breath," Gropper began. "You spend a lot of time at The Cabaret. That's going to stop, and you're going to find another place."

Baker's wind still hadn't come back, but as he hunched over, he was able to nod his head to suggest he understood.

"Good," Gropper said and started to head to his car.

Trapped animals are often unpredictable, so the fact Baker took a swing wasn't surprising. However,

Gropper didn't think Baker had it in him. It was one thing to prey on strippers, and it was another to retaliate against someone who had the upper hand. Gropper didn't take any more chances. He blocked Baker's effort and hit him with an overhand right which put him down. Gropper continued to walk to his car. If anyone wanted to get a closer look, Gropper hoped they would assume Baker was a derelict sleeping off a night of poor decisions. Gropper got into his car and went home.

The following morning, he took a seat at McGill's table and sipped the green tea which was already waiting for him. As usual, it was still hot. Since it was the weekend, he had arrived at the diner just before the church crowd had descended. He waited patiently at the front as throngs of families, including elderly grandparents with walkers and canes, situated themselves by the cash register. It wouldn't have made a difference when Gropper had gotten to the diner, as he wouldn't have to wait for a table either way. He'd caught McGill up on the end to their latest case, so McGill could get the word to Jennifer and assure her that her troubles would be over. He also advised McGill to alert the police to Mr. Baker, since working at an electronics store seemed like another red flag. After another minute McGill brought the conversation back to their current dilemma.

"Whoever killed O'Sullivan, if they were going to make a play for me, they're playing it close to the vest."

McGill paused to drink some coffee.

From the highway, Jesse Ames's office looked like a factory or an airplane hangar—a long, gray, rectangular building just off I-526 in North Charleston. There was a parking lot on one side and the Atlantic Ocean on the other.

Mark had spent two nights in the RRC. He was unable to sleep both nights due to a combination of things. He had been inundated with new rules and regulations. The RRC was monitored twenty-four seven which wasn't new to him, but it was different at the same time. They offered programs like anger management, money management, and parenting. He would have mandatory counseling meetings. The rules were strict, but not on the same level as he had been used to behind bars. Not to mention, he would still have to meet with Ames. It would be a brave new world, although, in some ways it was familiar. Still, that first night, he tossed and turned, read for a little, and when it was time, got up and put on his new suit.

Work looked like it would be promising. However, unlike his employment at the prison, he would probably have to follow through on his responsibilities. He had only gone in for the one afternoon, so far. They had made him a custodian at the library, which wouldn't have been his first choice, but it wasn't as if he had a choice to begin with. He was told if he did a good job, he could work his way up to being an assistant. It was a small step up in pay and responsibilities. It meant he could put down the mop and bucket. Instead, he'd have to stock the shelves, hand out library cards, essentially what he was supposed to have been excellent at doing in his former job.

That morning, he ate a quick breakfast from a takeout stand in a strip mall and took the 102 bus to his appointment with Ames. He didn't have a car yet, but once things settled down a little, he would check out some of the used jobs in his price range. He'd never been a car guy, not like this brother. If Steve had been in his position, he would have already spent hours looking for the perfect car. He probably would have remained in a garage the following few weeks giving it a tune-up, too. Mark never got that gene. He didn't care enough about it. As long as it got him from point A to point B, it didn't matter if it was foreign or domestic, old or new.

When he got to Ames's office, his shirt had soaked through from the humidity, but at least the office had air conditioning. The receptionist told him he would have to wait while she finished up with another client. He had assured the receptionist it was fine. All things considered, Mark had been able to adjust reasonably well. He'd heard stories about ex-convicts who'd gone crazy on the outside. They couldn't handle the freedom, even though they had thought it was what they truly wanted.

Mark had just begun to leaf through a magazine when the door to Jesse Ames's office opened, and a teenager in a tank top walked out. He turned around, lifted his fist in the air with his thumb and forefinger outstretched so it resembled a six-shooter, and when Jesse came to the doorway, he mimicked shooting the pistol at her. The kid even made the sound of the gun firing. She grabbed at her chest and played along.

"You got me," she said. Suddenly, she straightened up and all the playfulness was gone.

"I'm serious about next week," she said.

"Aye, aye, sheriff," the kid answered with an over the top southern drawl.

"I mean it," she said.

The kid blew imaginary smoke from his finger.

"I know," he replied. This time, the drawl was gone. The kid thanked her and walked out into the parking lot. Jesse saw Mark and waved him over. The melancholy look had lingered on her face, but she rid herself of it when he got closer. He followed her down the hallway to her office, one of many which looked similar to the others on the row. Inside was a desk covered in papers and folders. There was a file cabinet in the corner. From the looks of her desk, Mark didn't think she'd ever used it. Two guest chairs were unoccupied, so he took one of them.

"How are you settling in?" She said and rummaged through her purse. She removed a cellophane package, popped two gray squares into her hand, and began to suck on them.

"Fine," Mark answered.

"The library is good?"

"Yes."

She paused for a moment.

"Are you going to give me more than a one-word answer?"

"The library is good, and I'm settling in fine," he said.

Jesse sat back in her chair, and the springs groaned.

"This doesn't seem like it'll be a problem, but

I'm going to need to test you." She brought out some disposable gloves and a plastic cup from the top drawer of her desk. Mark nodded without saying anything, stood, and took it.

"There's a bathroom through that door," she said and pointed without looking up. She had already started to fill out a report form.

When he finished, he returned and handed her the cup. She stood from her chair, turned her back to him, and dipped the panel. Mark sat down in his chair. Her firearm was visibly clipped to her belt. He didn't know if she had done this on purpose or not.

"Okay, you're good," she said. She went to the bathroom, dumped the contents, threw everything in the trash, and sat back down. After consulting a yellow legal pad on her desk, she spoke again.

"I've got good prelims on you, so that's a good start," she sat back again. This time the springs in her chair stayed quiet.

"You keep this up, and it'll be smooth sailing," she added.

"You got it, sheriff," Mark said with a southern drawl similar to her previous client's.

He'd gambled, but she laughed. He laughed along with her.

* * *

"You sure you don't want none?" Paul said. He held an oyster shell in his hand and ran his thumb against the edge which made it wiggle.

"Yeah, I'm sure," Mark replied.

Paul slurped the oyster, discarded the shell, and squeezed lemon juice onto the next culprit. After he finished the preparations, he paused and took a swig of his beer. Mark did the same, although he was drinking sweet tea. He didn't think Jesse would violate him for drinking a beer, but he didn't want to chance it. Technically, he wasn't even supposed to be in a bar, let alone meeting with someone like Paul.

Paul had been working in Charleston for the last few years. He'd built a reputation as someone willing to get his hands dirty. Paul would do free-lance work for any of the local organizations, and word on the street was he was dependable. Paul ate one more oyster, wiped his hands on his napkin, and belched.

Mark didn't say anything. He wasn't here for the manners.

"So, business?" Paul said.

"Guy named McGill hangs out at a diner on—"

"Yeah, I know 'em," Paul said. He killed his beer.

Mark exhaled. He didn't like the tone of Paul's answer. Mark had learned in prison it was more effective to use a freelancer to handle difficult assignments. It provided a buffer in case of blowback. If Paul passed on the job, that would make him the third person in a row to do so. It seemed like no one wanted to touch this guy. McGill had a partner who kept a watchful eye on him. Mark had heard some rumors about McGill's partner, Gropper, and people's reluctance to make a play for McGill due to their association.

"Well," Paul began and raised his hand to get the waitress's attention.

Mark drummed the table quickly. He'd have to regroup now and come up with a new plan.

"I'll do it for double," Paul said.

Thinking that their business was essentially over, Mark, who had been shifting in his seat to rise, stopped moving and settled back down.

"What?" Mark said.

"Is that a problem?" Paul said.

Mark considered it for a moment. It would put a dent into his wallet, but it wouldn't cripple him.

"No."

The waitress came by. Paul ordered another dozen oysters and a beer. Mark was still good with his sweet tea, but he had a refill since it was free. When she left to put in their order, the two men went back to discussing the task at hand.

* * *

Liz knew, deep down, she shouldn't be snooping in Mr. Gropper's room. Her mother had told her she wasn't to go into his room if he wasn't in there. The euphoria of breaking the rules was too strong, though. Plus, she had already decided she wouldn't go through his things. She just wanted to be in the room. It was almost like he was there with her; it was hard to explain. He had become a close friend over the last few months. He never said no to a game of hide and seek, and he was good at it.

She would just spend a few minutes in his room. He would probably be home soon anyway. There weren't many times she was alone. Sometimes, for ten minutes here, or twenty minutes there; if someone who had been watching her had to leave before the next person could be there. Her mother wouldn't be home until late at night, so it was usually a neighbor unless Mr. Gropper was home.

Today, she had been with Tammy from next door, but she had had to leave early.

Liz looked around the room. There was a bed on the left side, against the wall, a dresser for clothes on the right, and a closet. Mr. Gropper had not put anything on the walls. The way he'd left it, the room didn't look like anyone lived there at all. She walked over to the closet and opened the door. She knew she should leave soon. She was disappointed there hadn't been anything. No clothes on the hangers and nothing on the shelves above. Although he was really nice, Mr. Gropper was a strange man. She was about to shut the door when she saw the key on the hook.

Had she not been looking closely, she would have missed it. Mr. Gropper had driven a nail into the wall on the side and a key hung from a lanyard. She removed it and held it in her hand. It didn't look like a key to any of the locks in the house. It had an orange piece of plastic at the end. A noise startled her from somewhere in the house. She put the key back on the hook and practically ran from the room. She no longer felt excited.

Paul's plan had been simple. He would only go inside the diner as a measure of last resort. For now, he was fine to wait in the parking lot in the comfort of his car. McGill would have to leave at some point, and Paul could take care of business then. He had covered all his bases. He had stolen the car, switched plates, and taken notice of where the cameras had been pointed in the parking lot. He could spray McGill with a whole clip and still be out of frame. Somehow, though, he knew it wouldn't be that easy. There was a reason most people would have passed on the job when they'd discovered McGill was the target. However, when Paul pulled this off, his rep would be enormous. He could probably even put together his own crew. A small voice in his head urged him to reconsider what he was about to do, but his desire to break into the game far outweighed the arguments this voice made.

The MP5 sat on his lap. Earlier, when he'd met with the dealer, it was one of a few choices in Paul's price range the man had laid on the blanket. The dealer had said the weapon just came back from Afghanistan, but he wouldn't go into more details. It worked well in close quarters, and the dealer had filed off the serial number, so it wouldn't be traceable. Paul spent more money than he would have wanted, but the weapon would suit any of his needs in the future. It was small, could be good for any distance, and could fire a ton of rounds. Recently, he'd been watching TV shows about drug cartels, and many of the assassinations consisted of people on motorcycles driving by and spraying an area with bullets. They preferred an MP5 as well. Much of the time, innocent people would be killed, and Paul knew that's what brought the police down. So, if McGill came out of the diner and went to his car, Paul would try to make sure no one else was in the vicinity. He wouldn't let the chance go by, but if he could help it, he would try to only attack McGill if he was alone.

Paul had been waiting in the car for about half an hour. He checked the time; it was close to midnight. That was fine; he wasn't in any rush. He figured he'd give it another two hours. If McGill didn't come out by then, Paul would put on the ski mask he kept in his pocket, go in, do the deed, and drive away. The junkyard would be closed, but Rico would be working the gate, and he'd let Paul inside. Paul would stay to watch the car get destroyed in the hydraulic press, something he'd always enjoyed, and then he'd head home for a good night's sleep. The following day, once word had got out, he imagined his phone would start ringing off the hook with offers. He touched the weapon on his lap and turned on the radio. Only a minute had gone by since he had last checked the time, so after he had looked at his watch again, he ordered himself to calm down. He had a plan, and it was a good one. Now, it was just time to put everything in motion. He was about to change the radio station to something more suitable when the driver's side window exploded.

* * *

A window punch is a small device the size of a C battery. When the button is pressed, the spring-loaded prongs deploy and can shatter the glass. These devices are used often used to rescue people from car accidents.

Gropper kept one on his key chain, and though he had never used it to rescue anyone, it had proven to be a very effective tool in his trade. The tempered glass had shattered inward. It distracted the man in the driver's seat who covered his face and let out a yell of surprise. The sound was cut short by Gropper, who nailed him with a Maglite. The man slumped forward onto his side, unconscious. Gropper looked around the parking lot. It was empty. He reached inside the open window, unlocked the door, climbed in, and pushed the unconscious man into the passenger seat. The man spoke gibberish as he was moved, but once he touched the far door, he stopped. Gropper sat in the driver's seat, shut the door, and found a jazz station on the radio.

Paul awoke in the passenger seat. His head ached. Not to mention, the radio was playing some sort of jazz music he couldn't stand. Most importantly, there was some guy in the front seat. Suddenly, it all came back to him.

"What the fuck?" Paul said.

The guy elbowed Paul in the ribs. The shot knocked the wind out of him. The pain had a delayed reaction, but he felt it coupled with the dull throb from his head.

The guy didn't say anything. It looked to Paul like he was listening intently to the music. Paul got the feeling if he said something to interrupt the music, the guy would hit him again. They both sat quietly until the song ended about a minute later. The DJ came on and spoke about the station's mission, fundraising opportunities, and the artists he would play over the next hour.

"Gropper?" Paul said.

The man nodded.

Gropper had taken the MP5, stripped it down, and threw the various components onto the floor of the back seat. He pocketed the firing pin. As he worked, he kept one eye on the man who moaned a little but remained unconscious for the majority of "Four on Six," by Wes Montgomery. The man stirred occasionally. Eventually, he awoke.

"What the fuck?"

Gropper threw an elbow to the unsuspecting man's side. The man absorbed the blow and winced from the pain. He got the message, and he stayed silent for the rest of the song.

"Gropper?" The man finally said when the song had ended. His tone wasn't one of fear, yet, but it also wasn't one of confidence either.

Gropper nodded in acknowledgment. Good, it would save him some time if this guy already knew who he was. Gropper put the car in reverse and backed out of the parking lot. They drove for a few minutes while the wind rushed into the open window. It helped to cut the humidity a little. It also made the music more difficult to hear, so Gropper turned up the volume. He remained alert in case the guy tried anything, but he got the sense the guy had resigned himself to the situation. Eventually, they pulled off into a dead-end street overlooking the Ashley River. Gropper shut off the radio. Outside, they could hear the sound of cicadas and the water.

"Okay," Gropper said.

The man twisted in his seat and threw a right cross, which Gropper parried, and hit the man with a back fist. The man shut his eyes and sat back. He brought his hand to his face.

"Shit!" he uttered. His eyes began to water.

"Are you finished?" Gropper said.

"Yes," the man replied. He touched the various parts of his face that were both stinging and swollen.

"I just have a few questions, and then you'll be able to go," Gropper said.

He turned the radio back on, but he lowered the volume. Gropper didn't think he would have to worry about anyone interrupting them, but he wanted to drown out their conversation regardless. It was a habit, and old habits died hard.

He looked forward but kept his peripheral vision on his foe. The man had a weary, pained look on his face.

"What's your name?" Gropper said.

The man paused for a moment as if he had to think about it.

"Paul," he said. Gropper nodded.

"Who hired you?" Gropper said.

Paul was silent again. He sighed.

"Can we make a deal?" Paul said.

"Sure."

"If I tell you who hired me, can you not say that I told you?"

This question caught Gropper off guard, but he maintained his composure. He decided he would never understand the priorities of some of these new guys.

"Sure," Gropper said.

"Guy who gave me the job is Mark Franklin; just got out of Lieber."

"Okay," Gropper said.

Paul continued with the story and relinquished all the details he knew. Gropper stayed silent. When Paul was finished, neither man spoke, though Paul looked like he expected something more. The disc jockey returned and introduced the next song, a classic from Miles Davis. The horns kicked in, and Gropper remembered better times with Miss Bradley. Then, he thought about Connie and Liz. Paul started to say something more, but Gropper put his hand up, so Paul stopped. Gropper listened to another minute of the song, and after another moment shut off the radio.

"So, now what?" Paul said.

"Well," Gropper said. He reached down between his feet and got his Maglite. He struck Paul on the collarbone and heard a crunch. Paul let out a yell, and Gropper struck him in the head, knocking him out again. Paul hadn't seemed like the type who'd seek revenge, but Gropper couldn't have him operational either. He opened the passenger seat and rolled Paul out onto the street. He drove a few blocks from the diner, wiped the car for his prints, and left it parked on the street. Someone would find it, or it would get towed. He walked into the diner, told McGill he'd be with him in a minute, and went to the payphone in back. He dialed a number for an EMS service and said he had driven by someone who'd been in the street and probably needed medical attention. He gave them the address where he'd been with Paul and hung up before they could ask him any follow-up questions. He walked over to McGill's table and sat down. A waiter brought over a green tea.

"Rough night?" McGill said.

McGill ate a few fries, drank some more coffee, and settled in so Gropper could fill him in on the details. The waiter returned and poured McGill some more coffee. At this time of night, the place was empty. Every so often one of them would glance over to see if McGill needed a refill. Most of their shifts would end soon, and the morning shift would take over. Gropper spoke of how he'd spent his evening with Paul.

"He a pro?" McGill asked.

"I don't think so. Just someone looking to jump a pay grade," Gropper said.

He continued with the story and revealed the name of Paul's employer.

"Guy named Mark Franklin," Gropper said.

"Franklin," McGill said.

"You know him?" Gropper said.

McGill drenched a few of his fries in gravy before he ate them. He chased it with more coffee.

"Maybe. Not personally, but I have an idea," McGill finally said.

"You think he'll make another go?"

"Yes."

They sat for another few minutes and talked about how to handle Franklin if this thing escalated. By now, the ambulance would have taken Paul to the hospital. He'd get a sling for the collarbone and some pain relief. Regardless, he'd be out of the mix for a while. Odds were, based on his plea to have some of the details left out, Paul probably wouldn't press charges against Gropper. It would have called too much attention, and the truth would come out as a result. Gropper finished his tea. He was going to return to Connie's for some rest, but he'd be back to sweep the grounds again later today. If this guy Franklin was serious, there was no telling the next time he might try again. McGill finished his fries, and the waiter came to take his plate.

McGill swirled the remnants of the coffee in his cup and watched it. When it settled again, he finished it off. The waiter refilled him, and McGill added cream. Gropper couldn't remember the reasoning behind adding cream at night but drinking it black during the day. Gropper stood, thanked the waiter, said he'd see McGill soon, and left.

He thought of the name Franklin; it was one he hadn't considered in a long time. Of course, it all made sense now. It had been early in his career. McGill had been a boot back then; a rookie who needed to be broken in. He'd gone through a rotation with a few partners, but ultimately, he had been paired with Ryan O'Sullivan who had been a good mentor. This had been before O'Sullivan had gotten his hand caught in the cookie jar. Or maybe this had been the incident which started everything. Either way, O'Sullivan helped prepare McGill for how things were out there. He taught him the ins and outs of the job, which had only been theory in the academy. Early on, O'Sullivan showed him important things like how far you could push a suspect without fear of getting blowback from the higher-ups, and how to work a CI. One of O'Sullivan's CIs had dropped a dime, which was what had brought them to Steve Franklin's house.

Steve Franklin hadn't meant to set up shop in Charleston. When he'd left New York, he'd had his sights set on New Orleans, but as with a lot of things in his life, he'd gotten waylaid with some friends who lived in Charleston. They'd sunk their money into renovating an old house and turning it into a coffee shop. They had convinced Steve to stay for a few weeks, which of course had become a few months. Steve worked at the coffee shop until he saved up enough money and chose a different gig. He didn't have the patience to be a barista. Instead, he decided to open a stall at The City Market. He started out selling odd knickknacks, and eventually settled on vinyl records which had been fashioned into bowls. In the short time, he'd owned the stall, it was the only item which had sold repeatedly. He never knew why, but he didn't question it.

He made a deal with a hippy artist from College of Charleston to knock out twenty or so at a clip. All he had to do was get this chick stoned, and she'd work for next to nothing. He had a nice hookup from the coffee crowd who, while they enjoyed their dark roasts, also enjoyed smoking weed. Eventually, Steve and the artist became an item. On weekends, they'd comb the vintage stores for cheap records. He would flip them for five to six times their worth to some unsuspecting bastard in from out of town. Those were good times, even if he was only scraping by. He didn't miss New York. He stayed in touch with his kid brother over the years. Jesus, Steve guessed he wasn't a kid anymore. In emails, his brother had mentioned how he was going to split from home soon anyway. Steve had understood Mark's frustration. The fear and restlessness were both things he had gone through. He told Mark he could stay with him in Charleston for as long as he wanted. Shit, Mark could even take a few shifts in the stall. Mark said he would take him up on it. Steve spent the next few weeks haggling with tourists and watching the locals sell sweetgrass baskets. It was accidental how he became a fence.

He'd been getting lunch at a place near the market and overheard two guys talking about how they were having trouble getting a good price for a car. Steve knew he should have minded his own business, but he couldn't help himself. He'd always been a gearhead, even back in New York. When he was still in high school, he saved up all his money, bought a 1940 Ford Standard, spending every free moment he had working on that car. It almost broke him to sell it, but he needed the money to escape. Besides, he sold it to a friend under the condition he would be able to buy it back someday. After he arrived in Charleston, he found a group who worked on cars. They did upholstering, restoration, detailing, anything anyone might need. Some of them also put in some time at a chop shop.

Before long, Steve had joined the men at the lunch counter and told them he could solve their car problem. That was how he became an intermediary for boosted cars. Once he helped these two guys, word spread quickly. The opportunity was too good to pass up. So, he would work at the stall as a cover, but he was no longer desperate for the income. He could make more in one night with his car business than he could in a month at the stall. He couldn't have cared less about the vinyl bowls either. The nights of sitting in front of the oven, watching the plastic melt, and inhaling possibly dangerous fumes—those were all things he was glad to leave behind.

McGill had only recently been partnered with O'Sullivan when a Jaguar with all the trimmings had gone missing. The owner threatened to raise holy hell. O'Sullivan calmly suggested he knew who to contact. Within a few hours, O'Sullivan's CI had given him Steve Franklin's name, and that's how McGill and O'Sullivan ended up at Franklin's house on an unofficial visit. Steve politely led them inside, and he seemed fine with entertaining their questions. It was a messy apartment, with some sort of classic rock coming from an antique turntable in the corner. Steve shut the machine off and offered them something to drink. When they declined, he grabbed a Coke and took a seat in a recliner. The living room was an eclectic mess of used furniture. O'Sullivan started with some simple questions, and they worked their way up to the missing Jaguar. Steve's response didn't shock them.

"Officers, I don't know what to tell you. I work at The City Market."

He looked at them as if while this would be a waste of everyone's time, he was still happy to oblige. McGill had taken a seat on the couch. O'Sullivan remained standing. His arms were crossed, and he stared at Steve.

McGill looked around at the various piles of junk in each corner of the room. Steve lit a cigarette and knocked his ash into a warped bowl on the table, which at one point had been a vinyl record. There were four others scattered about, probably filled with remnants of cigarette ash as well.

Steve went on to repeat the same line of defense every time they asked him a question about a stolen car.

"Steve," O'Sullivan finally said. He kept his voice level. "We know you've got a pipeline, and the problem is I've got a Jaguar that's gone missing."

O'Sullivan stopped talking but kept looking at Steve.

"What's that plate again?" O'Sullivan said without taking his eyes off Steve.

"138 S—," McGill started to say.

"138 SVX," O'Sullivan said completing the sentence. It was not the first time either of them had brought up the plate number. McGill didn't even have to look at his notepad anymore. He was beginning to get anxious, but he took a deep breath and reminded himself O'Sullivan knew what he was doing.

"See, this guy loves his car," O'Sullivan began. "He's called every day to see if we've found it," he added. O'Sullivan uncrossed his arms, began to walk around the room, and look at some of the pictures on the walls.

"I don't have the heart to tell him it's been torn apart," O'Sullivan said nonchalantly.

"Officer," Steve started to say.

"I know, you 'work at the City Market.'" O'Sullivan had now moved behind Steve who continued to smoke his cigarette, which was now almost down to the filter. Through it all, he had remained a cool customer. McGill had to hand it to the guy; he thought Steve would have cracked a while ago. O'Sullivan hadn't put the screws to him yet, but still. McGill didn't know if it would come to that. Although the guy who owned the Jaguar had a real hard-on for the car; not to mention, he was connected all the way to the top.

"Alright, listen," O'Sullivan began again.

Steve put out his cigarette and was going to light another one, but he decided against it.

"Yes," he said.

Even though he'd kept his composure the whole time, McGill could tell it had gotten to the point where they were on the verge of overstaying their welcome. The Jaguar owner's connections had given them some clout, but they couldn't color too far outside of the lines on this one. McGill needed to clear his head.

"Mind if I use your bathroom?" McGill said.

"Sure," Steve said, "down the hallway, second door."

McGill rose, nodded to O'Sullivan, and walked past him.

The bathroom needed to be cleaned, but it wasn't unusable. There was some sort of incense candle on the toilet along with a multipurpose lighter. Used towels hung over the shower curtain rod.

Must be laundry day, McGill thought. He finished up, washed his hands, and checked the time. He started to walk back to the living room. If they finished up here soon, they could beat the traffic back. He stopped in front of a bedroom. The door had been half open. He opened it all the way and went inside. The bed had been made. A gym bag rested on it. McGill could hear O'Sullivan and Steve talking. Against his better judgment, he opened the gym bag. He didn't know why he did it. They didn't have a warrant, and he couldn't have claimed exigent circumstances. Banded stacks of cash had been inside the bag. McGill couldn't estimate how much, but he made his play. He grabbed five; just enough so he could cram them into his pockets and they wouldn't bulge. He left everything as it was, returned to the hallway, and closed the door behind him, so it was open an inch. Shots rang out. McGill removed his service revolver, clicked on his radio, and called it in to dispatch.

"Shots fired," he yelled.

He raced back to the living room. O'Sullivan was in a weaver stance with his weapon aimed at Steve who lay on the floor. Blood had begun to pool around his body.

"10-31," McGill said into his radio, then remembered they had discontinued codes. "Suspect down, HBO. Send paramedics," he said again into the radio.

"Check 'em," O'Sullivan said as he holstered his weapon.

McGill cautiously approached the downed man. He'd taken a slug to the chest. The bullet hadn't killed him, but he would bleed out unless an ambulance got there soon. Steve held a .38 in his outstretched right hand.

McGill stared down at his empty coffee cup. He raised his hand into the air, and one of the staff appeared with a pot to refill him. He thanked the waiter and went back to his memories. The ambulance had gotten there in time, but Steve died once he got to the hospital. The owner of the Jaguar never got his car back. It had already been stripped for parts. The man was incensed, but his insurance took care of it. That must have been the end of the problem because the man never contacted them again. McGill never learned if O'Sullivan shot Steve Franklin and planted the weapon, or whether it was a good shoot.

McGill went before the board and testified to what he knew, so did O'Sullivan. He was exonerated of any wrongdoing by the IAD. McGill never brought the money up to O'Sullivan; whether the man would have chewed him out or happily taken his cut was a mystery but one McGill could live with. It wasn't until after their partnership ended that O'Sullivan was indicted on a few felony counts during a separate internal affairs hearing. McGill managed to get away with a hundred fifty thousand dollars. It lasted for a while, and with his business acumen, he was able to stretch it.

McGill and O'Sullivan remained partners for another few months after the shooting then O'Sullivan rotated into a different department. That was when he began to get into trouble, or so McGill had heard. Very quickly, McGill became a seasoned veteran who knew how to break in the new boots himself. He would go on to amass a crew of capable CIs, one of whom, Renee, he became close with even after he'd retired from the job.

It was only a few years after the Steve Franklin shooting that McGill decided he'd had enough of the job. He wasn't even close to the twenty years needed to retire on a half pension, but that was fine. He could find something else to do.

He took another pull of his coffee and saw he was down to the dregs already. He waved the waiter over; he didn't put the cup into the air as it made him feel like royalty. The guy filled it again.

"Thank you," McGill said. The guy nodded and made haste. With his current arrangement with the owner, McGill would never pay for a drink or a meal. However, at the end of each day, he would leave a sizable tip for the waitstaff. The phone rang. McGill went to the back and got it on the third ring. It was the desk sergeant from Vice whom McGill had called earlier and told him to look into Baker. The sergeant told McGill they had served a warrant on Baker and found a treasure trove of illicit videos on his hard drive. Forensics was busy combing through them as they spoke. They were going to charge him with a laundry list of things. He thanked McGill again and wished him well. McGill assured the desk sergeant it was nothing. He hung up the phone, returned to his table, and made a mental note to let Gropper know the update. Then, he went back to thinking about his current problem.

Mark hung up the phone. Paul had just regaled him with all the details of his attempt on McGill, which included Paul's trip to the hospital. He told a believable story of being attacked by McGill's associate. Paul claimed he didn't give Mark up at all, but Mark doubted it. Mostly, Paul rambled on about how even with a broken clavicle, he wouldn't go against his code. Mark told Paul he believed him. However, he knew he would have to make certain Paul wasn't lying. Typically, Paul would have been at the bar on an evening like this one, but now that he was out of commission, it meant he would probably be at home.

Outside, the humidity was still thick, but Mark had already begun to get used to it. There was nothing like being in the outdoors again with the freedom to move around, even if the heat made things uncomfortable. Mark was going to take full advantage. He would only have to stay in the half-way house for another few weeks or so. It wasn't so bad. Since he didn't have a drug problem, the staff wasn't in his business all the time.

Mark walked the few blocks from the RRC to the bus stop. Eventually, the 30 bus came. He paid the fare, took a seat, and thought about the plan of action. Had he expected someone like Paul to be able to pull it off? It just went to show him how desperate he must be.

Before he knew it, enough stops had gone by, and he was near the oyster bar. He pressed a button to alert the driver who pulled over. Mark got off at the bus stop and walked another few blocks to Paul's house. He stepped onto the porch and heard the sound of the television coming from inside. He knocked.

"Yeah?" Paul said.

"It's Mark."

Paul didn't respond. Mark figured Paul was probably trying to decide how best to play it. Mark wasn't going to give him the chance to think of anything.

"Come on man. I'm dying out here."

Paul had gotten closer to the door; when he spoke again, he sounded suspicious. "What do you want?"

"I felt bad on the phone," Mark said. "I thought I could get you a sixer and a few dozen oysters. What do you say?"

Mark readied himself for Paul's refusal and had started to think of another excuse to get inside, but Paul had already begun to open the door.

"Sounds good," Paul said. "Come on in. 'Scuse the mess."

Mark walked past Paul and into the living room. It looked like it was all IKEA furniture. Paul took a seat on the couch. The television was on, but the volume had been turned down. On it, a talking head was getting animated about the Gamecocks' basketball team, and whether they would have a chance to make the NCAA tournament this year.

"Do you want me to call for delivery?"

Paul took the cell phone from his pocket. He probably had their number on speed dial. While Paul was busy, Mark had reached into his own pocket and grabbed a tube of pepper spray. He'd picked it up a few days back. He'd never given pepper spray its due. It had always seemed to him to be something reserved for would-be muggers who preyed on old ladies or skateboard punks who pulled pranks, but he'd seen a video about how awful it was to experience it on the receiving end, and he became an immediate convert. Not to mention, it was only about ten bucks at any gas station. Here in South Carolina, it was completely legal.

The first stream hit Paul in the forehead. He adjusted and managed to get Paul in both eyes.

"Jesus, What—" Paul had started to say. Then, the pain and disbelief hit him simultaneously. He scrunched his face and emitted a low roar. He tried to wipe his eyes, and the pain of moving his arm with a broken clavicle caused him to cry out. Mark walked into the kitchen and returned with a carton of milk and a dishtowel.

"So, listen first then answer, okay?" Mark said.

"Okay," Paul said in between sniffles.

"If I like your answer, I'll wash your eyes with milk. It's supposed to help."

Paul dry heaved a few times. His nose had begun to run uncontrollably.

"Okay," Paul said again. He had begun to hyper-ventilate.

Mark soaked the dishtowel in the milk, walked in front of Paul, and rubbed it across his face.

Paul had not been expecting it, so he drew back.

"Did you give me up?" Mark said.

A beat went by.

"Yes."

Paul braced himself for a follow-up attack, but nothing came.

"Relax, I'm just confirming what I already suspected," Mark said.

Paul started to dry heave again.

"Jesus, you got a fan?" Mark said.

"No," Paul said and spit on the floor.

"I'm going to open a window."

Mark walked behind the couch and opened a window to air the place out a little. Paul continued to shake on the couch. Not satisfied, Mark went into the kitchen and turned on the ducts above the stove.

"I don't know if that'll help," Mark said. Paul continued to shudder and drip fluids of various kinds. Mark asked another few questions and applied the towel. When he was satisfied he had all the answers he needed, he placed the towel and the milk in Paul's hands. He told him the effects would wear off in a little while, but he shouldn't rub his eyes. He left Paul a pitiful mess on the couch.

"You're getting better," Gropper said after he had bent down to look under the bed. Liz, who had been lying on the floor under the bed, hadn't moved, even after Gropper had spotted her and said his piece. Her eyes were closed, but she had a large smile on her face.

"Can we play one more time?" she said finally and opened her eyes.

"Sure," Gropper said. "One more time." Although, he knew one could easily become two or three. When he'd first moved in, if you'd have asked him about how he would have chosen to spend his downtime, it certainly wouldn't be playing hide and seek with a child. Regardless, she had been getting better, which had become a source of pride for him.

Long gone were the days of listening to records with Ms. Bradley, but this wasn't so bad. Liz slithered out from under the bed, hesitated in thinking about where she could hide next, and did a sort of stutter step.

The memory returned without giving Gropper any warning, and suddenly he was back underneath the bed in the motel, watching the Latino hitman kill two prostitutes who had been bound and gagged. Gropper hadn't thought about them for a long time. The sight of Liz emerging from her hiding place had brought back this unwanted memory. Gropper put the thought from his head.

"Listen," he began, and the girl stopped moving. "I know you went into my closet."

She looked like she was going to launch into hysterics, which would either precede a denial or an excuse. Gropper put his hand up to cut her off before she could say anything.

"It's okay," he said, and that seemed to calm her down.

"Just don't go in my room," he said. He didn't know if he was inviting further investigation into his life by saying this, but she looked ashamed enough to steer clear in the future.

He put his arm around her and hugged her. He didn't know what to expect, but like with most things, she had already forgotten about it. She was busy looking around the room to find another decent hiding place. Before she could assume a new spot, both she and Gropper heard Connie's key hit the lock of the front door. Liz tore from Gropper's arms and raced out of the room. He waited to give them some time together. Connie worked late most weeknights, so the weekends were the only time she and Liz got to see each other. During the week, Connie was asleep when Liz left for school, and she was at work when Liz went to sleep.

From the tone of her voice, it didn't sound like she had come home early due to a problem. Liz said she had been in the middle of playing hide and go seek, and she told her mother she was going to go hide again. Gropper heard Liz's feet echo off the floor as she ran away.

"Have fun," her mother called out to her.

Gropper walked into the living room. Connie had already gone to her bedroom to shower and change. He was by himself.

"Hey, Liz," he said aloud to the empty room. He knew his voice would carry throughout the house, and wherever she had hidden, she would still be able to hear him.

"Let's pause the game. I want to talk with your mom for a few minutes."

She didn't respond, but Gropper assumed she had heard him. Gropper took a seat on the couch and waited. He heard her moving around in her bedroom. Liz popped her head out.

"Okay," she said. She shut the door. Gropper had already suspected where she would hide, but he didn't want to ruin it. Another ten minutes or so went by, and Gropper enjoyed the silence. Connie finally emerged from the bedroom. Her hair was still wet, and she had changed into sweats. She smiled at Gropper, went to the kitchen, and came back with a glass of wine.

"Remember that kid I was telling you about weeks ago, the one with the ruptured aneurysm?" she said.

"Yes," Gropper said.

She took a seat, sipped her wine, and relaxed.

"He's going to make it," she said.

"That's great," Gropper replied.

"Yeah, the odds were not in his favor." She started to describe some of the things which had gone wrong, and her story quickly entered the realm of jargon. Gropper understood most of what she talked about. Ultimately, they moved away from that conversation to discuss more philosophical concepts, a subject Gropper felt more comfortable with. Before he knew it, a half an hour went by, but Liz hadn't come out of the room. Either she had forgotten about the game, or she was being respectful of their privacy. Gropper excused himself, walked over to Liz's room, and knocked on the door.

"Yeah," came from inside.

Gropper opened the door. Liz lay on her bed, reading.

"Think we could pick up our game tomorrow?"

She answered without taking her head out of the book.

"Sure," she said and flipped a page.

Gropper shut the door and returned to the living room. He sat down.

"Thank you," Connie began. "For everything. Liz, listening to me—"

"It's my pleasure," Gropper said before she could finish. They continued talking for a few minutes. Gropper said he needed to leave, and Connie turned on the television.

McGill touched the outline of the scar on his chest. He could barely feel it through the material of his shirt. It had been a while since he had had to do any legwork, and he didn't miss it. He'd played the game for long enough, and he'd been good at it, but he also recognized when it was time to hang it up. Thankfully, Gropper wouldn't have that problem; he was made for this line of work.

McGill sat back down at his table. A pizza burger deluxe awaited him. He began to mix some mayonnaise and ketchup for the fries. His side of sliced avocado, to add more greens to his diet, sat next to the plate of fries. He picked up the burger and began to help himself to his second course of the evening. The phone rang.

Mark had trouble staying calm, but he forced himself. He'd only been in the parking lot of the diner for a few minutes. McGill was probably running late. Earlier, Mark had gotten a friend of his from the RRC to call McGill and set up a meeting. His friend said she knew McGill only met people at the diner, could he come to their house instead since her mother was bedridden? McGill had agreed without any provocation and told her he would be happy to make an exception. They set the meeting for later that evening. It had been a simple arrangement, and it had only cost Mark his dessert for the next two weeks. He was happy to comply.

So, now he waited in the parking lot. It was already dark out. He'd finally concluded that if he was going to take care of this situation with McGill and finish getting retribution for his brother, he was going to have to do the job himself. Whereas O'Sullivan had been practically gift-wrapped, McGill was turning out to be much more difficult. He couldn't believe his luck when he had discovered he and O'Sullivan were housed in the same prison. He wasn't a spiritual man by any stretch, but he swore a higher power must be involved somehow for that situation to come about. However, perhaps the same deity had felt things had been too easy for Mark, so now he was setting things right by making McGill a much for a difficult opponent. Mark exhaled and reminded himself not to get carried away. He forced himself to go over the plan one more time.

McGill would leave the diner momentarily. He would go to his car, at which point Mark would accost him, put two in his chest, and one in his head. He'd seen the move used by special forces soldiers in various movies. It was known as a failure drill or Mozambique drill. It was the only way he could be sure to take the man out and finally end this thing.

Gropper tilted back his Jack and Coke. Like McGill, he'd also cut back, but there was still something relaxing about indulging every so often. He sat at the table in the back near the kitchen. He could still see the entrance clearly, and he could fully relax. The place would fill up later once the college kids had exhausted themselves at the bars on King Street. In the meantime, it was still early, so Gropper had the place to himself. Charlotte, the bartender, was busy reading a paperback. Per Gropper's request, she had put a jazz playlist on the sound system. Eventually, as the place filled, she'd have to put on top forties, but for now, she could cater exclusively to Gropper. He'd become a regular over the last few months, and he tipped well. Gropper finished his drink. He'd allow himself one more and listened to a few more songs.

At one point, Gropper thought of visiting John

and Ms. Bradley, but if someone had been watching him, he didn't want to reveal any connections to his former life. So, he took solace in thinking they were doing well. He knew at Ms. Bradley's advanced age it would be dicey, but he chased the thought from his head. He also thought of the time he had spent in Hong Kong. It seemed like a lifetime ago. Gropper checked his watch; he could have one more and would still have time to make it to the diner.

The front entrance to the diner opened, and McGill stepped out into the parking lot. He looked like he'd put on some weight, but Mark could tell it was him. He watched McGill take his time walking across the parking lot to his car while balancing a full cup of coffee. Mark opened the car door and stepped out onto the asphalt. He shut the door behind him. His pistol was out, and he kept it low. He walked toward McGill and felt unstoppable. McGill had placed the cup on the roof of his car and was busy rummaging around in his pocket for his keys. Mark got within forty feet, then thirty. At twenty feet, he stopped. McGill was so engrossed in what he'd been doing, he hadn't noticed.

"Hey!" someone yelled from the edge of the parking lot.

The shots echoed in the dark and shattered the stillness. There were three in total, and Mark took them all in the chest.

McGill lowered his weapon. He flicked the safety on and put it back in his holster. He hadn't gotten used to it, and the holster constricted him since it had been at least twenty pounds ago since he'd worn it. He nodded to Gropper who had emerged from the edge of the parking lot.

"Thanks," he said.

"No problem," Gropper replied.

Both men walked to the front of the diner. McGill popped his head inside where the staff had begun to gather.

"Everything is okay, but can one of you call 911?" McGill said.

The staff looked like they wanted to ask a ton of questions, but they also knew if McGill had wanted to give them more information, he would have. Plus, if they waited another half an hour, they would know everything anyway. They all took out their cell phones, but McGill suggested only one of them call, so it wouldn't overload the system. A waitress began dialing the numbers, and everyone else put their phone away. McGill walked back outside and took a seat on the asphalt next to Gropper. He had left his coffee on the curb, so he picked it up and took a sip.

ACKNOWLEDGMENTS

A huge thank you to my family for their support, and to Ralph and Bill for reading an early draft and giving me feedback.

Andrew Davie received an MFA in creative writing from Adelphi University. He taught English in Macau on a Fulbright Grant. He's also taught English and writing in New York, Hong Kong, and Virginia. In June of 2018, he survived a ruptured brain aneurysm and subarachnoid hemorrhage. His first book *Pavement* was released in July of 2019 by All Due Respect Books. His work can be found in links on his website: asdavie.wordpress.com.

BOOKS

On the following pages are a few
more great titles from the
Down & Out Books publishing family.

For a complete list of books and to
sign up for our newsletter,
go to DownAndOutBooks.com.

The Girl with the Stone Heart
Scott Grand

All Due Respect, an imprint of
Down & Out Books
November 2020
978-1-64396-122-4

Winter has set in a small town on the California coast and a fishing vessel has been lost amongst the gray waves. Grace runs the bowling alley and ghosts through his own life. He lives in the layer of fat between the underbelly and society.

Grace is charged with issuing payments to the fishermen's widows. He pulls on his funeral suit and borrows his grandmother's New Yorker. When Grace is unable to find one woman, he uncovers something that threatens the oligarchy's reign and his way of life.

Don't Shoot the Drummer
A Lou Crasher Novel
Jonathan Brown

Down & Out Books
November 2020
978-1-64396-150-7

A security guard is murdered during a home robbery of a house tented for fumigation and Lou Crasher is asked to solve the murder. The rock-drumming amateur P.I. is up for it, because his brother Jake is the one asking. Lou fights to keep his musical day job and catch the killers.

When the bullets fly he hopes all involved respect his golden rule: Don't Shoot The Drummer.

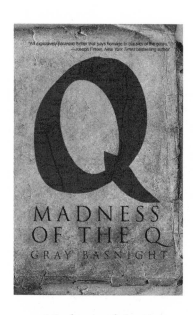

Madness of the Q
A Sam Teagarden Thriller
Gray Basnight

Down & Out Books
April 2020
978-1-64396-088-3

Humble math professor Sam Teagarden is plunged into a global crisis of religious bloodshed sparked by discovery of the Q Document, an ancient parchment uncovered in northern Israel.

Allied with American agents, he soon finds himself alone, trying to save the maximum number of lives while struggling against an international gauntlet of paranoia and blind religious zealotry.

Deemer's Inlet
Stephen Burdick

Shotgun Honey, an imprint of
Down & Out Books
August 2020
978-1-64396-104-0

Far from the tourist meccas of Ft. Lauderdale and Miami Beach, a chief of police position in the quiet, picturesque town of Deemer's Inlet on the Gulf coast of Florida seemed ideal for Eldon Quick—until the first murder.

A crime and a subsequent killing force Quick to call upon his years of experience as a former homicide detective in Miami. Soon, two more people are murdered and Quick believes a serial killer is on the loose.

Made in the USA
Middletown, DE
04 January 2021